"The Celebrity Series"

The Good, The Bad and

The Two Cookie Kid

Story By Shirley Kelley
Illustrated By Jimmy Claridy

Better Place Publishing

Cheshire, Ct. 06410

Everything We Publish is Manufactured with the Earth In Mind!

To Doc Justin and The Two Cookie Kid!

SONG
Written by Eric Herbst
Performed By Johnny Cash and
The Better Place Band :
    Andrea Herbst - Backing Vocals
    Russ Gordon - Guitars
    Ron Ciaburri - Bass
    Chris(Sweet Jam) Morrisey - Drums
    Don(Mo-Jo) Destefano - Harmonica
    Mark(West) Marusa - Steel Pedal
    Jerry Capuano - Piano
    Eric Herbst - Guitars
Engineers - John Murphy, Rob Cavalier, and
    Richard P. Robinson
Recorded at Better Place, LSI & Trod Nossel Studios
Produced by Eric Herbst
Special Thanks to Johnny Cash, and
    Def American Recordings.

STORY
Written by Shirley Kelley
Narration by Johnny Cash
Intro Narration Andrea Herbst
Edited by Sheri
    Gloria Genee
    Eric Herbst
Musicians :
    Russ Gordon - Guitars
    Don(Mo-Jo) Destefano - Harmonica
    Jerry Capuano - Piano
    Ron Blouin - Piano
    Eric Herbst - Guitars
Digital Editing - Richard P. Robinson
Special Assistant - Justin Corris
Assistant to the Assistant Dylan Herbst
*The story was based on the origional song by
the same name.

"The Celebrity Series"

The Good, The Bad and

The Two Cookie Kid

Story By Shirley Kelley
Illustrated By Jimmy Claridy

Better Place Publishing

Cheshire, Ct. 06410

Justin and Wally played cowboys in their backyard while they waited for Grandpa. The boys looked forward to Grandpa's visits. Their friends did too.

Grandpa was a cowboy in the Old West.
He would tell his stories while they sat
by the campfire in the backyard.

"Was this how cowboys spent their nights?" asked Jo, when they were gathered by the fire. "Yep, the very same way," said Grandpa. "Did they have comic books?" asked Chip. "Did they listen to the radio?" Tiffany asked.

"Nope, folks in the Old West told stories by the campfire,"
said Grandpa. "Did they have cookies?" asked Wally.
"They sure did! Now that reminds me of a story..."
The children grew quiet as he began his tale.

When I was a boy in the Old West, there was a little town by the Rio Grande. It was called Cookieville. It was quiet and friendly. There was a saloon, a bank, a barber shop, a bakery and a general store.

Everybody knew each other, and no one ever broke
the law. Sheriff Buster and Deputy Jo spent most of
their time riding, roping and target shooting. They
needed lots of practice.

One day, folks started noticing all their cookies were gone. No one knew it then, but that was the day the Two Cookie Kid came to town. The Kid was wanted for cookie robberies all over the West and Cookieville was next on his list.

The Kid held up the stage coach and made off
with the delivery meant for the general store.

His next stop was April's bakery. "Put all the cookies in this here bag," the Kid demanded. Miss April did not move. He picked up a giant jelly doughnut and said, "Don't make me use this, Miss."

April turned to run for the door. The Kid squeezed the
doughnut and grape jelly oozed all over her new apron
and stuck her to the floor. He grabbed a big bag of
cookies, whistled for his horse, Oatmeal, and rode
down the dusty trail.

The Two Cookie Kid was emptying every cookie jar in Cookieville. He stole the cookies from every lunch pail in the schoolhouse. The children cried and cried. "Just drink your milk," their teacher said, but the children knew, milk without cookies just wasn't right.

Doc Justin was robbed of the cookies he prescribed when people got hungry in between meals. "There are going to be a lot of grumbling stomachs without those cookies," said Doc Justin.

The Squeaky Door Saloon was owned by Miss Tiffany. She ran a strict business. There was no spitting, no bad words, no hair pulling and you had to wipe your feet before you came in. A slow game of Old Maid was being played at the corner table. Chip, the piano player, was practicing for his next music lesson and at the bar, root beer floats were served all around with cookies on the side. The saloon doors squeaked loudly as they swung open.

Squeak, squawk, squeak, squawk. The Two Cookie Kid walked in. "Ma'am, you should fix those doors," the Kid said to Miss Tiffany. Miss Tiffany stared at him. "I don't want no trouble here, Kid," she said. "I run a respectable place." The Kid grinned. "Let's have some music, piano man," said the Kid. He threw a cookie that knocked off Chip's hat. "Y-y-y-yes sir, but I only know one song," Chip said as he began to play Twinkle Twinkle Little Star.

The Kid walked over to the corner table and sat down. He shuffled the cards quickly and dealt a hand. "Looks like I win!" the Kid exclaimed. "You cheated," said one of the players. "We all have the Old Maid." The Kid just smiled as he gathered all the cookies in the saloon. "Let the chocolate chips fall where they may," he said as he walked out of the Squeaky Door Saloon. Squeak, squawk, squeak, squawk. The Kid gave Oatmeal a cookie before riding off.

A large crowd of town folk had gathered at the jail. "Sheriff, we need your help," they pleaded. Sheriff Buster had accidentally locked himself in the jail cell and Deputy Jo was still untying herself after steer roping practice. "Sheriff, you have to do something," said Miss April as she let Buster out of the jail cell. "The Kid stole all the cookies from my bakery and I'll never get the stain outta this apron."

"How am I gonna cure all those hungry stomachs?" asked Doc Justin. "Every cookie jar in town is empty and the Squeaky Door Saloon has just been hit." Sheriff Buster and Deputy Jo went to visit Miss Tiffany at the Saloon. The crowd followed.

Squeak, squawk, squeak, squawk. "Miss Tiffany," said Sheriff Buster, "If you don't mind my saying, you really should fix those doors." "Then I'll have to change the name of my saloon," said Miss Tiffany. "Do you know how much a new sign costs, Sheriff?" She put her hands on her hips. "Now, what are you going to do about the Two Cookie Kid? He's bad for business. He didn't even wipe his feet before coming in. Cookie crumbs everywhere ... Where's the law? Where's the justice?"

"What we need is a posse," said Sheriff Buster. "Now who's going to ride?" "I'm late for my piano lesson," said Chip as he scurried out the door. Squeak "I've got house calls to make," Doc Justin said. Squawk

"I have to soak my apron," said Miss April. Squeak
"I have to finish untying all these knots," said Deputy
Jo. Squawk "I have to fix the saloon door and paint a
new sign," said Miss Tiffany.

Suddenly, in walked a man all dressed in black.
Squeak, squawk, squeak, squawk. Everybody gasped
and took one step back. The Man in Black said,
"I'll find those cookies and I'll bring them back."

Sheriff Buster helped him load the stage coach with empty cookie bins. "If he's hiding in those mountains, this will bring him down," said the Man in Black.

The Man in Black was ready for a show down at high noon. As the stage coach got out to Crooked Creek, he saw the Kid.

The Kid was standing in front of the stage coach and said,
"Step down from there, Mister, you know what I'm here for.
Gimme all them cookies, and hit the floor."

The Man in Black said kindly, "There are no more cookies Kid, just these empty bins. You're going to have to share the cookies with us, Kid, or I'm gonna bring you in."

The Kid got really quiet. He looked at the Man in Black. The Man in Black stared back. After a long staring match, the Kid said, "Well, I'm all outta milk anyway, so you win."

He lead the town folk to the cookies he had hidden in the mine. It was the biggest cookie strike since the rush of forty-nine.

They loaded up ten wagons and before the job was done,
the kindly Man in Black rode off into the sun.

"Grandpa, that was a great story," said Buster.
"What ever happened to the Kid?" asked Wally.
"Oh, he went on sharing cookies all
over the West," said Grandpa. "Did
you know the Two Cookie Kid?"
April asked. "Yep," said Grandpa,
"Knew him well." Crunch, Crunch.